Field Notes

Shorts

·

Stories
&
Essays

Darren Hawthorne

Field Notes

Copyright © 2024 by Darren Hawthorne
ISBN-13 979-8-218-56482-7

Cover Design and text formatted by Watercress Press

Published by the author

Printed in the United States of America by Ingram Spark and distributed by Ingram.

Contents

Field Notes

Endeavor to See Beautiful Things

Endeavor to see beautiful things. I like the idea of there being half of me that is inherently loving, tender, and kind. An Anima. A part of me that sees and is drawn to beauty. That maybe even is beautiful. I think of Emerson in the woods, his dim pulpit-god transforming, under the trees, into the big blue-sky God. Or Whitman walking along the docks marveling at the wooden ships arriving from around a vast world. Kerouac walking alone across American (in his best moments) looking for something he probably never found. Etheridge Knight with a little bag of dope in his pocket wanting to feel at home with his family, then leaving because his bag was almost empty. The name of a relative long gone, who nobody remembers except grandma, written in a family bible. The beautiful things.

When does evening end and night start? Somewhere, after dark, after dinner for the ones who work during the day. After sitting, after smoking. After trips to the store if those are necessary. Maybe it happens while we watch tv and we don't notice. Whenever it happens, it happens and, for me at least, it comes with a sense of the inevitable. It's night and tomorrow is coming. If I'm tired, I go to sleep. If I'm not finished with something, I'm disappointed. If I'm not tired, I worry and dread the hours ruminating, thinking, the morning coming (too) slowly through the darkness.

On rare nights though, the crust of the earth opens, quietly and slowly, and smoke floats gently out and fills and covers everything, the room, the house, the streets, the neighbor's houses. It gets in my eyes and I can't see very well but it doesn't matter because I can make everything out with better clarity and my eyes closed. It gets in my lungs and makes me aware of my breathing, forcing me to take slower and deeper breaths. I go out the front door to the street and look up and down the rows of houses expecting to see all my neighbors out there gazing into the cracks of the earth and surrounded by smoke. I walk out in the backyard and look up into the sky. Sometimes there's a moon, sometimes not, the black shadows of owls and nighthawks move against the sky. Plumes of smoke curl up into the night.

Darren Hawthorne

Cats, Vultures, and a Long Life

Overhead, the vultures circled, very high up, but getting lower with each round after round. A committee of vultures. A Murder is what a flock of crows is called, not vultures but it could be used here too. A murder of crows, a flock of crows. A flock of vultures in flight is called a 'committee' or a 'kettle'. A group of vultures feeding on a carcass is called a 'wake'. The world is a place full of life, I've always known this and can see it now more clearly than ever. I'm lying in the tall green grass and things are biting me that I can't scratch with these old legs and claws. The sky is blue with beautiful white clouds suspended peacefully, barely moving. And, of course, the small, but getting larger, black specs of the vultures circling. Other birds occasionally cross my field of vision, but they're not interested in me, I'm too big. An old cat laying in the tall grass. I've spent most of my life skulking around, staying undercover, sleeping during the day and hunting at night to avoid being snatched by a hawk or an owl, hunting things that live in the grass and the trees; snakes, mice, squirrels, and of course birds. I have a pretty low success rate with birds unless they're baby birds who haven't learned to fly. Don't misunderstand, I've stalked, captured, and eaten plenty of birds but they've always made a difficult meal.

Do vultures kill things? I don't know. It's also funny that I'd never wondered about that until now. I know they eat dead things, but I don't know if they'll finish me off with some kind of coup de grace or wait for me to depart naturally. I could try to crawl off but how far would I get? And where would I go? I was already hiding under a pile of downed branches until I heard the familiar (and terrifying) rattle of the snake's tail and burst out of there using the last of my energy, running and dragging myself to where I am now. (Still). Laying in an empty overgrown lot. The sun is hot and it's only late morning, even if the vultures don't come for me, I don't think I'll last the day. I can hear the bees buzzing from one flower to another all around me. They'll make their way back to their nest before sundown by a mysterious homing instinct to drop their nectar payloads and vibrate through the night with their hive and queen.

I've spent my life living at the house across the street. When I was just slightly older than a kitten they started putting a bowl of food out for me in the morning so I decided to make this place my hunting ground. I would eat a couple bites but leave most of it as bait for other things that I preferred more, birds and squirrels mostly. They would come to the bowl to steal a few pieces of dry food and that's when I would pounce. Not always though, sometimes I'd let them take a few pieces, as much as they wanted even. I'd watch them from a hiding spot and delight as they'd sneak up to the bowl, scared, looking nervously around, steal a few pieces and scurry or fly away as if they'd got away with something. As if they'd beat me or won. They didn't get away with anything. I wasn't hunting that day. They could have sauntered up to the bowl in any manner they chose, and I would have let them live. I'd have them when I was ready.

It happened a few times that another cat would find their way into my the neighborhood and locate my food bowl. I'd have to fight, and I did, every time. I lost more fights than I won but I always fought and that kept any interlopers from settling permanently in my area. It's one thing to win a fight but it's another to have to fight every time you're hungry; in the end they'd decide it wasn't worth it. They'd move on. I never went into the people's house but sometimes they'd come outside and pick me up and comment on my wounds or a missing piece of my ear and say things like 'he was protecting his food', 'he doesn't like to share', silly things like that. I was protecting my food, but not the food they gave me. I was protecting my lair. I always preferred fresh meat, blood, crunching bones, even coughing up feathers was enjoyable to me. It reminded me of the hunt and the kill. It reminded me that I am a cat. A wild thing. That this is what I am made for.

I started thinking about the vultures again, wondering if they'd make this quick or just let me die from thirst or the heat. I was considering whether I'd fight them when they came. I suppose I'd have to, not because I had any chance of winning or even wanted to make them pay for me as a meal, but because I wasn't sure how I could cross over if I didn't. I was also aware I wouldn't have much time to feel one way or another when the time came, but with whatever short amount of time I was granted I wanted to be proud. I also didn't want to die. That may sound like a silly obvious thing to say but it came as a bit of a surprise to me that even here, having lived a long life and with no hope of surviving I didn't want it to end. I was ready to die. I'd accepted that it was going to happen (and soon), but I didn't want to die. At the same time, I knew there was nothing I could do about it. I wasn't getting sentimental or emotional. I didn't experience some kind of deep wave of empathy for the things I'd baited and eaten. I didn't experience a bunch of silly regrets. None of that. It's just that I wanted to keep living.

They were much lower now, and I suspect they were beginning to realize I didn't pose much of a threat. I'd spent my life watching from hidden places, first moving very slowly, stalking my quarry, then moving very quickly, pouncing, clawing, biting, taking my prey's life by surprise and eating their flesh.

They were even closer, I could smell them now and they stunk. I never stunk. I stayed clean. I had my pride. They had landed and were walking towards me with their wings spread wide to appear larger, more intimidating. Their strange heads jutted forward. Watching me. They paid me no respect. I was reminded these were not hunters, they were scavengers. They had no stealth or pride.

And I had nothing left. I played dead (it was surprisingly easy). I'd spent my life being still and pouncing at the exact right moment. I thought I'd try it one last time. I waited for them to get close, waited for them to get comfortable. They would take a few steps forward, then jump back, scared, testing to see if I'd jump up and attack. They did this for a few moments, it was hard for me to quell my instinct to attack but I did. I stayed still, even letting one of them peck at my stomach without moving. Finally, when two or three came closer, satisfied that I would offer no resistance, I poised myself to jump up and get one. I didn't think I had the strength left in me to kill it but maybe I thought, I could retain some dignity by defending myself, and also purchase myself a few more moments. The bees were buzzing in the flowers, the grass was waving gently in the breeze, the stink of the vultures was close. I was numb to the heat and the biting things from the ground. I picked the one I'd go for, he seemed to be the least careful of the three and I thought if I was quick enough, I might just get to his throat. He came in close and I tensed my muscles making ready to attack, anticipating his skinny neck in my teeth , his blood on my tongue. I couldn't do it! I couldn't spring! I could barely move. They knew their trade and had judged my state better than I had. He came in slowly; his carelessness hadn't been reckless, but experience and confidence. Then came his two partners, I hissed but they didn't even move. They started pecking at my eyes and stomach. I tried to turn my head, tried to claw, hissed, but it was over. I was done.

Sky Ship

On the desert floor; cactus, jackrabbits, sand, small rocks of every color, and me, standing in awe of a mountain range in the distance and above all of us, getting closer, a rolling wall of dark gray, nearly black, clouds. The mountains, some peaks covered in snow, others disappeared into the clouds. Where I was, several miles distant and thousands of feet lower, everything was still. A light wind blew and the creosote, ocotillo, palo verde started to move, barely visible. A jackrabbit sprang from beneath a cactus, ran off about 25 yards, and disappeared under the cover of another bush. Perhaps the breeze or movement startled him; maybe I did.

The sky above me was still cloudless and blue, but the quality of the light was getting dimmer because of the approaching darkness. The breeze picked up, getting stronger. The plants and bushes were now in continuous motion. The whole desert floor was moving. Here and there, jackrabbits abandoned their refuges and went looking for another, quieter, safer place. There was none.

Over the mountains a great wooden ship appeared. Small at first, and I thought I must have been seeing things, but as it got closer, there was no mistake, it was a large wooden ship with oars sticking out the side moving forward and backward, rowing towards me, digging into the atmosphere in perfect rhythm. The ship was making its' way directly towards me. I was afraid, of course, anyone would be. I heard a man shouting; there were no words or language I could understand, Ho! Ho!, Ho! he yelled in time with the oars. I didn't move, whether because I couldn't or didn't want to, I'm not sure. The ship rocking side to side approached.

As it got closer to me, it lowered to thirty feet off the ground or so, came to a stop, became still, and a wooden gangway was lowered to the ground. When the gangway hit ground a woman, large and extravagant, started walking, spinning, and dancing soundlessly down the ramp towards the ground. Jackrabbits started coming out from their hiding spots everywhere and running towards the gangway. They ran up the plank and into the wooden ship passing the women, neither taking any notice of the other. This woman's presence, though she descended quietly and gracefully, was in no way calming or reassuring. A force moved in front of her and around her, I could feel it, and it was frightening and unfamiliar.

She came to the ground and walked towards me stopping a few feett away then turned towards the mountain, the dark clouds, looked up at the blue sky and made some kind of yelling or howling noise, that echoed across the desert and seemed to go out into and across the world. The world felt it, I was sure of that. Nothing moved but everything swelled and got larger or seemed to. Everything grew. In retrospect, I'm not sure if she made any noise at all, but there was a calling and an answer from the mountains, the clouds, the wind, the desert, the plants, and every other thing.

She walked up to me and looked into my eyes. She was horrible, beautiful, terrifying, her skin was blue, white, black, green, and every other color imaginable; her hair was long and black. Her eyes were fire. She pulled out an old flintlock style pistol and shot me right through the chest. I was thrown back onto the ground. She laughed as the echo of the gunshot died in dessert. I could feel my heart being torn to pieces, my lungs expelled any air they held, my ribs broke and shattered as the bullet passed through me. It exited my back and tore a large chunk of my spinal cord out with it. I lay in the sand and pebbles dying. She stood over me and put her booted foot directly on my chest and stomped down, the pain was unbearable. She laughed. I tried to push her foot off but I couldn't budge it; she was too strong and I was too weak. She laughed more loudly, then took out a long knife, bent over me, and began to hack away at my neck. I was sure she was trying to decapitate me, and I couldn't stop her. I lay there writhing, feeling the pain, my mind awake to every strike and slice, but my body unable to move, to save myself, to stop her. My head came free and as it rolled away with my eyes still intact, I could see first the ground, then the sky, then my body lying on the desert floor, then the ship floating in the sky, then the jackrabbits, and accompanying it all, I could hear her hearty boisterous laughter. The wind picked up drastically, I could see the whole desert moving, every bush, tree, desert scrub back and forth in the wind. From the ship's galley I heard the oarsmen cheer, laugh, and hoorah.

She picked up my head by my hair and with her strong arm tossed it up into the sky and straight through an opening in the side of the boat. The rowers screamed and laughed in ecstasy. They jumped up from their benches where they'd been watching, grabbed my head and started tossing it around. There were men and women here of every size, shape, and color. There were no chains, these were not slaves, these were free people pushing the ship through the sky of their own free will. They held my face up to theirs, crossed their eyes at me, stuck wet fingers in my ears, held my nose closed and put their hand over my mouth, pinched my cheeks, and howled with laughter. Jackrabbits were everywhere around their feet, on the benches, even climbing on their shoulders and heads. One woman rower pulled my tongue out of my mouth, further than I thought possible, and used it to swing my head around in circles before tossing me over the heads of her companions. The cheering got louder. A man picked up my head by the ears and pointed me outwards with my eyes facing forward. He walked to the edge of the ship and held my head over the side pointing down so I could see my body lying on the ground.

I was dismayed to see that the woman had taken her knife, cut open my chest, and pulled my damaged, shot through heart out of my chest and was stomping on it. She started doing a dance in her heavy brown boots, smashing it to mush on the ground. My body lay there, headless, motionless.

The galley cheered louder than before for as long as it took the woman complete her dance. Suddenly she was done. I don't know how she knew I'd had enough but I did, and she stopped. Her long hair blew in the violent winds. She stood still and looked around the desert bush then towards the mountain range and the dark clouds. She took everything in, she ingested it. In the galley the cheering stopped, there were a few more lone yelps and hollers but before long there was no sound other than the wind and the rustling of the bushes. The man holding my head over the side dropped me. I landed on the ground with a thud, rolled, and came to a stop where I could see the woman walking back up the gangway plank to the ship. As she strolled upwards towards the ship, deeply breathing in the air the jackrabbits began descending the gangway. The woman and jackrabbits passed each other again, without acknowledgement. When the jackrabbits reached the ground they all bounded off in different directions and disappeared back into their desert. The gangway retracted back up into the ship, the door closed, the ship banked and started back in the direction of the mountains.

I jumped up and ran to my car. It didn't start right away but eventually did and I drove away as quickly as I could. I watched the ship in the rearview mirror get smaller and smaller in the distance. As I sped down the potholed caliche road towards the highway a jackrabbit ran in front of the car. I felt a small bump as the tires rolled over its' body. The thought of stopping crossed my mind but I quickly decided against it. As I looked in my side mirror, I saw the rabbit jump up, stand on its hind legs, and shake his paws at me. His mouth was moving, yelling something but I couldn't hear what he was saying.

Homeless Prostitute

She was walking down the sidewalk in the bright light of a Sunday morning carrying a bundle of clothes and high heeled shoes, like a baby, tight to her chest. A lace bra, half unbuttoned blouse, and men's underwear is all she wore. An unusual sight for this neighborhood.

•

Both my daughters graduated from college yesterday (Saturday). A day full of parties beginning at 8:30 a.m. with all their friends over at the house for breakfast, the living room filled with balloons, ribbons, and noise. Then on to the ceremony. Everyone dressed in long gowns and high heels, hair done, perfumes, and makeup. Afterwards a backyard pool party, food, cigars, and music. Then an expensive restaurant for dinner. Then graduates and friends all went out for a night of dancing.

•

She looked like she might have been crying. There was nowhere to hide on a sunny Sunday morning. I wondered why she didn't at least put her dress on.

'Should we help her?', I asked my wife.

'No', she said.

I drove past her.

'She's going to get in trouble,' I said, 'someone is going to hurt her. I'm going to help her'.

I turned around, pulled up to her, and asked her if she needed help. She walked over to the truck.

'Yes', was all she said and walked around to the passenger side of the truck. My wife lowered the window, they looked at each other for a brief moment.

'Can I get in?' she said impatiently, indignantly.

My wife opened the door and let her in the back seat.

•

Everyone woke up late this Sunday morning but they were all back at the house by 11am. Coffee, tacos, laughs, everyone dressed in sunhats, sunglasses, beach shirts, they were all going to have a day of floating and swimming at the river. They hung around, made a lot of noise, and complained about one of them who still hadn't shown up because she drank too much last night and was late. The last one finally made it and with their big colorful bags packed full of sunscreen, speakers, phone chargers, fruit, crackers, and more they made their way out of the house and into their cars. Then they were gone. Silence. An empty house.

•

'Are you ok'? I asked.

'I got kicked out of a hotel, she said, 'can you take me to Walmart? Fuck! I can't go back to the hotel!' She was animated, rambling.

'I need to go back to Ohio. Do you know where Worklodge Inn is on Perin Beitel and 410?'
I hesitated before answering, not sure if she was really looking for answers.

'I think I know, isn't it by...' I started to say,

'I need to do some shopping.' She interrupted me, she wasn't listening at all.
I was having a difficult time following what she was talking about.

'By Diamonds, the strip club. Do you know it?'
Again, neither my wife or me answered.

'They won't hire me there. Fuck that place, it's a dump.'
She was quiet for a minute.

'Fuck! I don't have any money, but I need to get back to Ohio.' I think it's by Paradise. They won't hire me at that one either. She was jumping from one topic to another. She was still high from whatever she'd done the night before or this morning.

'Fuck! I don't know how I would've got here. I think it's over here.'
She was pointing out the back window. I started to pull into the parking lot she was pointing towards.
'No take the turn-around! Somewhere around here. I've got my stuff there in one of the empty rooms. There's some people I can stay with there'.

•

We dropped her off in the Worklodge Inn parking lot. It looked like the hotel had been closed down for a while. Broken windows. Broken asphalt. Fully clothed people sat in plastic chairs around an empty swimming pool.

•

My daughters came home not long after dark, sunburned, tired, smiling, and proud. Their friends helped them bring all the stuff inside the house and left quickly – everyone was quieter than this morning. The four of us went outside and watched the lunar eclipse.

Incarceration

A beep, a pause, another beep, then an automated lady's voice telling him to hold a moment. 'She'd better pick up.' he thought. Every time he called, he worried she wouldn't pick up, that she wouldn't accept the charges, that she wouldn't want to talk with him, that she'd leave him alone in this place. It's just county jail so relatively safe, but there's too much time. Time to do nothing. Time to lay in bed. It's one large room with rows of bunk beds lining two of the walls. The other wall is the phone bank and the entrance to the restrooms. The fourth wall is made of glass with guards sitting behind it all day. A TV hangs from the ceiling in the middle of the room and guys watch from the rows of metal tables and benches that are bolted to the floor. Fluorescent lights, the din of the tv, and everyone dressed in orange. Too much time. Time to think. Thinking is something he's not very good at, though he thinks he is. He knows how to con, strategize, plan, manipulate, read people, identify the weak and needy, how to create confusion and use people to get his needs met. He calls this thinking but it's all really just a hustle and thinking at a level no higher than a spider or house cat. The truth is he's not very good at even these skills, if he was he wouldn't be dressed in the county orange calling his mother collect at 10:30 in the morning on...what day of the week was it? He doesn't know.

Another beep and he hears his mother's voice say,

"Hello" a question and timidity in her voice. Of course, she knows who it is, she had to accept the reverse charges.

"It's me" he says. Then silence for a moment. He says nothing more and she waits for him to say something. After a short time she says,

"How are you?"

"I'm fine". he says impatiently, already beginning to feel annoyed by her. Does she think he can't handle himself? "Don't worry about me. I'm ok. What about you? Have you talked to anybody?"

"About what?" she says, knowing exactly what he's talking about but desperately trying to avoid the question

"About what!?! What do you think I'm talking about!! About what! The fucking lawyer, Mom! The fucking lawyer! Have you talked to anyone about getting the money to pay the fucking lawyer! Fuck! It's the last thing we talked about last night and the same thing we talk about every fucking day! Have you talked to anyone!" He can feel the anger in his chest and his head. It feels better than the fear and the boredom that he's always feeling. It feels like he's doing something.

"Oh. That." she says, quietly.

He can almost see her looking at the floor or out the window as she says 'oh that'.

"Oh that?! Yes of course that! Jesus fucking Christ, Mom! I'm stuck in this fucking shit hole. What the fuck do you think I'm calling about! I mean fuck! What the fuck is wrong with you? Can't you fucking help me! Call somebody. Julianne. Aunt Janine. Your boss! I don't know. Just try somebody!" The anger has him now. He's savvy enough to keep his voice down to a whisper and a hiss. This is county jail so there are not many fights but when someone starts yelling and screaming and acting out of control they'll get checked. The need to keep his anger under control focuses it more directly into the phone, through the line, and into his mother's ear.

Though she's frightened the whispering and hissing join them together into a conspiracy. A warm, familiar feeling. They each have a job and she hasn't done hers. It's her and him against the world. A world that's constantly trying to keep them down and crush them both. It's been this way since he was a kid and she was a young mother. Back then it was her husband, his father, that was trying to crush them both and they were co-conspirators trying to survive his tyranny and drunkenness. Or it was the teachers at school who wouldn't let him take things from other kids or insisted he keep his hands to himself with the girls. Or the mall security guards who pressed charges when he stole shoes. Shoes he didn't need but wanted because they were a style his friends had and he didn't. Neighbors who caught him spray painting on their fences and would throw him to the ground and once, one of them even spray painted his face. After these incidents and others, he would go home and his mother, terrified, indignant and angry, would talk about how everyone was against them. His father, the schools, the police, the neighbors, the system. 'The whole thing was rigged' she would say, as she cleaned his face, or talk about how prissy the girls at school were, or what 'do-gooders' the neighbors were or how he deserved the same shoes as everyone else.

Only now she was older, and so was he. He was in his 40's, she in her 60's. She'd never had the singular moment, or revelation, or awakening about the situation they'd been in their whole life, but dimly she'd begun to wonder. He'd been in and out of jail so many times over the years, would he ever figure it out? Was there something wrong with him? What was wrong with him? Why is he the way he is? Even his father, technically still her husband, (they'd never divorced though they hadn't seen each other in twenty years), violent and dark as he was, worked and kept the lights on. Her son had two babies with two different women, *her grandchildren,* whom he had nothing to do with and she'd only met a couple times. She had worked her whole life, paid off a small house, kept a car running, all these things by herself. Her husband had moved on years ago and she'd never got involved in another relationship. She'd always been convinced her husband was their problem and as far as she was concerned when he left, the tyranny ended. She wondered why her son didn't see it.

On the phone she was numb. And silent.

"Are you there!?" he asked, in an impatient sarcastic tone like she was a small, stupid child who refused to answer.

"Yes, I'm here." she replied steadily, answering just the question, not the insult.

"Well, that's good I guess." He said in his best demeaning tone.

He's tapping his finger against the mouthpiece of the phone loud enough that she can hear it like a rapid drumbeat in her ear. His thoughts and actions are all unconscious. He's constantly in a state of such deep discomfort inside that his only conscious thoughts are only those that serve to ease the pain. He doesn't know he's in pain, has no point of reference, and wouldn't care if he did. He's never felt 'good'. The drugs, the stealing, the women, the violence, they're all distractions that require very little effort beyond the hustle and produce nothing more than forgetting. But forgetting what? That's a question he hasn't asked himself but still it's there, dimly, just like with his mother, small and distant doubts tug at him. When these happen, he lashes out. At anybody. If there's nobody there, he goes through the list of people that have wronged him. Father, mother, teachers, police, friends, girlfriends, the government, the system. It's better if there's someone in front of him, a girlfriend, someone weaker, he can work on. Someone from whom he can take what he needs and dismantle them in the process. Someone he can berate. Someone he can hit. There's always someone available for that role and they always manage to find each other.

"I'll try." she says finally.

"Yes try. Holy fuck! Please." The 'please' was not politeness but exasperation and meant to remind her of how dumb and incompetent she is.

"Please!!" he said again implying the reason she hadn't been able to find the money he needed was because he forgot to add this nicety to his request. That she was too stupid to act without being begged. In that single word he made everything her fault, put the responsibility for his all his failures on her.

She accepted it.

"I'm sorry...I'll call your sister or ask my boss." A soft whimpering silence. "I think I have vacation pay that I can collect. I'll ask my boss tomorrow."

"What! We've been talking about this for two fucking weeks! What the fuck! You have vacation pay? Why are you just now saying 'I'll ask tomorrow' he said imitating her voice in a whimpering and pathetic interpretation. "Jesus Christ I've been sitting in here for two weeks with these fucking losers. Are you kidding me? What the fuck is wrong with you? Ask him tomorrow and don't forget! Fuck!" Hiss. Hiss.

"You're right. I'm sorry. I won't."

"Please!" he says again.

"I'm sorry. I will. I will."

"Great!" He says. He can feel the anger coming down. Here's a chance, something to hope for. "That'd be great!"

She can hear his finger tapping faster.

"How long will it take to get? If you ask tomorrow will they cut the check tomorrow? What day is it anyway? Tell them you need it right away. It's an emergency."

"I'll try. It's Tuesday" she says, hearing the excitement in his voice and feeling better. She's not thinking about her lost vacation time or her job, only that he's calming down and sounds happy.

"Man, that'd be great! Can you ask today?"

"No. The boss is out today." nervously.

"Fuck! No big deal though. If you get the money tomorrow you could leave work early and get me out of here tomorrow. I'd be out before the weekend! That'd be great! You think he'll give it to you tomorrow?"

"I don't know. I'll ask. Maybe. I'm sure it'll be no later than Friday, sometimes they only cut checks on Friday's but I'll ask." she speaks rapidly to the beat of his finger.

"Friday! Fuck! Friday! Fuck him! Tell him you need it tomorrow. Tell him it's an emergency. Fuck him. You've been at that company forever! They couldn't even stay open if it wasn't for you. Fuck them. Tell him you need it tomorrow! Friday?!? Fuck that!"

She answers quickly, desperate to keep him happy,

"Ok tomorrow. I'll tell them it's an emergency and I need it tomorrow."

"Perfect. Perfect." He said. "Thank you! Jesus! Finally! Fuck! thank you." The anger was going out of his voice, and she thought she even heard him exhale a deep breath of relief.

She exhaled also. This was love, taking away his hurt and fixing his problems. Whether she got the money, or even asked for the money, if he was still in jail tomorrow or next week, if he got out and changed or didn't change, if she ever got to see her grandchildren, none of it was really important. All that mattered was that he was feeling better and therefore, so was she. She got a little flutter in her chest. She did good and he loved her, she could hear that in his voice. He stopped hissing at her and calling her names and that was love.

"Tomorrow sweetie, tomorrow we'll get you out."

Pursued

The three of us had been together for a long time. She and I since she was a baby. Him, I'd always known, but he didn't start tagging along with us until a while back, I don't remember exactly how long ago, but it had been some time, and here we were, being chased, running again.

It was difficult getting her up the ladder, but I pushed her hard and made her go as fast as she could. He followed behind us but, truth be told, I wasn't too concerned about him. She didn't understand the danger we were in, and I couldn't blame her. I'd been telling her for so many years that everything was going to be ok, I shouldn't have been surprised that she believed me. Without question, everything was *not* going to be ok. I pulled the ladder up after us and whispered to them to be still and quiet. She was smiling, I think she was just happy to be with me, He looked confused. He was getting close to the end of his long, adversarial, and contentious life, so it was hard to tell if this was his dementia or just more of his stubbornness. She'd been born with mental and physical disabilities but had always been a pleasure to be around and I'd always taken care of her. I'd often wondered if I did it out of love, duty, or if it just gave me something to do to keep my mind off myself. I never really answered the question. As far as he was concerned, I only took care of him out of a sense of duty. He'd been born with all his faculties and hadn't done much with his life but be a thorn in the side of others, still I couldn't bring myself to cut him loose; so, he became mine also.

They'd been after us for a while; when I think back, it seems like forever, but for exactly how long, I couldn't be sure. What I knew for certain was they'd been after us all afternoon. A couple hours before, I looked down the road and, from a distance, I could see them coming. I was disappointed, scared, and angry, but not surprised, I knew they'd eventually come again. There were about 20 of them, carrying clubs, cheering each other on, and staying together in a loose group formation.

I got them both and we started running (such as it was) out the back door. I had to carry her. She hadn't grown in stature past that of a 5-year-old even though she was 20 and I'd been carrying her on my back for most of her life, so, for both of us, this was nothing new. She knew how to hold tightly to my neck, and she'd never fallen off. I had to hold his hand and pull him along. We were being chased. I was being chased. Nobody needs to think about what to do when they're being chased, they run. We ran. It came naturally, an instinct hard-wired into us all the way back to our one celled ancestors, somebody chases, somebody runs. This is the natural order. We ran (slowly) through the backyard and into the woods. It wasn't a very deep wood but I knew we could lose them there and that before long, if I picked the right paths, we'd come up on an old empty house I thought we could hide in.

They were a group of people, men, women, even children. That there were children there scared me most of all, their presence meant the adults had no doubt in the righteousness of their cause. They wanted to show their kids the right way of doing things. Either that or they were so lost in their fury they didn't care. In any case, I knew if they caught up with us, there would be no mercy. I couldn't hear them anymore as we stumbled through the woods. I reasoned that we'd gain some time and a good head start since they would search the house, the outbuildings, and so on for us. There was the possibility they'd just put a match to it all, but I didn't think they'd do that; they were too bent on malice to show us that mercy. I was certain they wanted to witness our suffering rather than have us simply burn and disappear in a fire.

I remember old paintings of fox hunts. The colors were always faded, men in red outfits riding horses, dogs bawling through green fields and trees. The scene was always chaotic. I've wondered how the dogs didn't get trampled, how the riders stayed in mount, how the participants didn't shoot one another, and so on. The whole affair looked so desultory; I've never understood how the foxes ever got caught. I was running through the woods hunted by a group of people who I knew would kill us if they caught us and I couldn't help thinking about those paintings. What did the foxes do to deserve such a turn-out, kill a few chickens, steal a couple eggs? Did the dogs and the hunters out-hunt and outsmart the fox or did the fox just run out of energy, give up, and get caught? When the fox hid in his shallow borough, did he believe he was safe from the hunters and their relentless pursuit?

Relentlessness, that's the thing. An individual stands no chance against a crowd. Something happens and they won't stop until they get the recompense they're after. They had their minds made up, I wasn't a person to them, I was an idea that didn't fit with their own. Likely, they hadn't given it that much thought. They didn't know me, didn't know who I was, and didn't care. They were coming for me and they believed in their cause and that was all that mattered. The mindlessness of bureaucracies. In the past I've always thought of 'the system', 'the machine' as something codified; the military, the department of motor vehicles, the city permit office, people in desks behind people in desks following a list and doing what they're told, following procedure. I never thought of a bureaucracy as a large angry mob hunting me through the woods in the late afternoon, but I had a suspicion that this was exactly who was chasing me (and us). A mindless group of people doing exactly what they were told and manipulated into doing.

We plodded along until we came out into the clearing I'd been looking for. It was an overgrown field with a small abandoned house at the edge of the unkept field, and that's where I thought we could hide. When the owner sold his farm to a developer, he'd hung on to this house and a small piece of land with the hopes his kids or grandkids would someday want it, but nobody did. Surrounding it was a neighborhood full of new houses that were much larger and more modern than this old, dilapidated place. My hope was that the mob would think we went straight to the main roads to catch a bus or something and wouldn't think us foolish enough to come here. Plus, I doubted they knew of this place, only by mistake would they come across us.

We went in through a broken window and found the entrance to the attic. I pushed her up the ladder, let him follow, and pulled the ladder up after us. The holes in the roof let in enough light to create shadows so we moved back into the darkness, hid, and I whispered and threatened them to be still and quiet. She thought we were playing a game and kept snickering. He sat there looking confused and angry, turning his head in all directions trying to figure out what was going on. Over an hour had gone by, it was starting to get dark, and I was beginning to think we were going to make it. The attic insulation was making the back of my neck, face, and chest itch insufferably. I imagined huge cotton-ball like wads of insulation all over the back of my neck and face. I kept trying to rub them off with my hand and it kept coming away clean – there was nothing there. The invisible fibers were mixing with my sweat, running down my back and chest and driving me crazy. I could see they were bothering her also; she wasn't snickering anymore and was also rubbing her face and head trying to get it off. The place was saturated with the stench of animal urine and feces. I wasn't sure how much more I could take. He thought it was his shirt that was making him itch so he'd taken it off, even though I whispered to him to stop moving. Now he had black insulation all over his damp back and was grunting and violently scratching the places he could reach.

I could see flashlights and hear yelling coming through the trees. I'd miscalculated, they'd found us. Of all the ways we could've gone, I'd figured this was our safest option. If I'd been alone, this isn't the way I'd have gone but given my traveling partners inability to move quickly, this was the best I could come up with. They'd found us now, I could see the lights at the edge of the clearing and knew it wouldn't be long. They were coming through the field, and I knew it wouldn't take them long to figure out where we were. I told them both we had to go. He started fussing about his back and I saw that he'd dropped his shirt in a pile of animal waste and insulation. She was starting to cry, maybe from thirst, maybe from heat, maybe the smell and the itching, I didn't know. I didn't know what to do. I angrily whispered to them to shut up. I crawled to a hole in the roof, poked my head through and watched the men and women in front with the flashlights coming through the field. I went back to them and told them again, to shut the fuck up and that we had to go right now. They both continued itching themselves and crying. I went over to him and tried to help him with his shirt but he kept pushing my hands away. I went to try to pick her up, but it was getting dark, she was in panic, and I'd startled her; she slapped me with both hands.

I backed away from them both and looked at their barely visible outlines in the dark. The reality of the situation, already deep within me, sunk unavoidably deeper and I knew this was the end. I looked towards the other side of the attic where there were enough missing roof boards to get out and get away before the wolves got to us, but I didn't know how to do it with those two. I looked back towards them, and I could dimly see him frantically waving his hands and hear her crying getting louder.

I've heard people talk about decisions they've made in their life say things like, 'I didn't even think about it at the time', or 'I didn't know what I was doing'. I wish I could say something like that. I knew exactly what I was doing. I knew that if I left them there, they'd be found and the murderous posse would stay busy with them long enough so that I could get away. Anger came up in me and I was indecisive, overwhelmed; 'why the fuck do I have to take care of these people?' 'Who put me in charge?' 'It's not my fault these fucking losers can't take care of themselves!' thoughts like this. I didn't even say goodbye. I stood up and ran stooped over across the attic joists towards the hole in the roof at the other end of the house. As I was scurrying over a fence into the subdivision, I looked back and saw the snarling face of a lioness, lit up by flashlights dragging the shirtless old man across the grass in her teeth while the others tore at his legs and arms. I didn't want to see what they did to the girl. I turned my head, jumped the fence, and ran.

Accident

I was looking at my phone trying to find the audio book I've been listening to. It's a sweet little love story about a married woman ignored by her husband and by her college aged son. A silly story and certainly no more than a fantasy, but something to listen to besides the miserable news or the old songs on my play list while I drive home from work. I was thinking about stopping to get a pizza or McDonalds for my husband and myself and I was going to call him as soon as the story started. I wanted to catch him before he put on his virtual goggles headset and started playing his video games, or 'Gaming' as he calls it. After that, he's gone. He'll still answer the phone but when I ask him what he wants all he'll say is 'I don't care'; if I suggest a few different places, he'll just respond, 'whatever'. I have his orders at the different fast-food places memorized so even when he doesn't tell me where he wants me to stop, I know what to get him when I do. God forbid I don't order correctly or they mess up his order and I don't catch it before taking it home. Once he texted me five times while I was at work because they didn't put cheese on his spicy fried chicken sandwich the from night before. The night before! I ordered it correctly, I always do, and I could have double checked it before I left but I was in a hurry, there was a line, it was raining, and plus I checked the receipt before I pulled away and it said 'spicy chicken with cheese'. What else am I supposed to do? And besides, fuck him. I mean I love him and I'm glad he's there when I get home, but really, fuck him. He texted me 'it just shows you don't care about me', 'you don't care about me enough to take two seconds to check if they got the order right'. He lives in my house. After my first husband left me (my son's father), I swore I'd never get put in a situation like that again. My son and I would've been homeless if it wasn't for my grandmother letting us stay with her. Finally, I bought a house and had it when he and I met. He was living in an apartment with two friends splitting rent and it didn't take long before he moved in with me. It made sense since I couldn't leave my son alone, a toddler at the time, to be with him. I took care of the house, my son, and him very well. He was only working part time then so I got him whatever he needed. Eventually I convinced him to get a real job and work full time.

He works in customer service for a cable company. I worry about his health but at least I'm happy. He's able to work from home since all he does is answer phone calls from seven at night till three in the morning from people complaining about their bill or having technical problems and transfers them to the correct someone who can help. It's a national call line so he has to pick up the time changes across the country, hence the odd hours. I worry about him though because he spends nearly all day gaming with his virtual reality headset on and all night answering the phone staring at the computer with his earpiece in. Between his video games, his work, and sleeping I don't know if he gets up at all except to go to the bathroom. That's why I can't understand when he complains about something so stupid as getting his order wrong. He doesn't have to do anything! I have to get up and go to work, deal with people, get dinner every night on the way home, and so on. He gets to sit there all day and does whatever he wants.

Anyway, I was looking for my audio book on the phone when the accident occurred. The collision was powerful and fast and I didn't know what was happening. It felt like my eyes and body stayed in the same place but were also spinning around and I was in several places at once. My head hit the driver's side window and it was like hitting a brick wall, the glass didn't break, and then the airbag smashed me in the face pushing me back against the seat. I remember looking up right before the other car hit me and seeing the other driver's face, eyes and mouth wide open.

It was all over in an instant and then I was facing in the opposite direction. Everything was still and quiet. I sat there experiencing a sort of vertigo for I don't know how long, not more than half a minute, but probably less. I looked around and tried to get my bearings on the situation. I understood I'd just been in a car accident, but I couldn't figure out where the other car had come from, if I was hurt, and if I was, where, and so on. The side of my head hurt but as good as I could determine, I wasn't bleeding anywhere. Somebody had opened my door and was looking in my face, 'are you ok? Are you ok?' he said. I looked at him and after a brief second said 'yes'. He stood there holding my door open and then a lady came over and asked him, 'is she ok?' They mumbled for a moment, probably about me, until I started to get out of the car. 'Take it easy' one of them said. I did not like this at all, spinning, loud noises, air bags, people talking about me, telling me what to do. Again, 'Take it easy.' 'I'm ok' I said tersely and got out of the car. I was dizzy but took a step or two before realizing I was missing a shoe. I went back to the car, found my shoe, slipped it on, and walked towards the front of the car. By now there were three or four people there, walking around, looking, one of them was on the phone. I turned around to walk towards the rear of my car and nearly ran into a tall, slender, dark-haired man.

He looked me in the eyes and very gently said, 'ma'am, are you ok?' I looked at him and didn't answer. 'Ma'am, I'm a doctor.

Are you ok?' A doctor? How did he get here? He was handsome, dressed well, tall, slender, closely shaved, and well put together, he must be a doctor. The shoe I'd just put back on was loose and I stumbled. I reached out and caught myself on the side of the car, he took my other arm. 'Come over here and sit down'. He led me to the parking lot next to the car and helped me sit down. He told me to be still, looked in my eyes, and asked me a few questions, 'what's your name, what day is it, who's the president' things like that, then said, 'I think you're ok'. I held on to his arm, it felt good. He felt good. I asked him how he got here so quickly and found out he owned a property nearby and was driving past. I'm not young anymore but I'm attractive enough, dress well, and take care of myself. I wasn't surprised by his attention, and I forgave him right away for his interest in me. After a moment, he said he wanted to check on the other driver and got up and walked away. I stood up and went back to the car, walked around it and gathered a few things from inside. I could hear sirens getting closer. I looked towards where the doctor and the other driver were standing and noticed he wasn't holding their hand or looking into their eyes. They could have been talking about something as silly as a video game. He came back to me, looked closely into my eyes, and once more asked if I was ok. I said 'yes, just a little overwhelmed'. He stayed on the scene for a few more moments until the police arrived. Before he got up I got his name. He went to the police, they talked for a moment and he left.

My husband worked in a call center for an insurance company prior to his job with the cable company so he considered himself an expert on insurance claims. For the next week he told me over and over again that it was my fault, that I wasn't paying attention, that I never pay attention. He said it was a miracle I hadn't already killed somebody with my driving. I told the police the other driver was speeding, but my husband wouldn't let it go. I got contacted by an accident lawyer and told him the other driver was speeding, and so on. We were going to sue the other driver but the police lied and said it was my fault. They said I'd pulled out into oncoming traffic without looking. I was looking! Yes, I did look at my phone, but first I checked to see if traffic was clear before pulling out. The police always lie. And of course, the other driver was a man so that didn't help either. The lawyer stopped returning my calls. My husband kept on about it. I guess he wanted me to admit it was my fault but it wasn't and I wouldn't. After a week or so he finally stopped talking about it and went back to his video games.

I wanted to thank the doctor for his help so I did a quick search and found his office online I thought about it a while and decided to personally deliver a box of cookies. I had a meeting that morning at work so I dressed a little nicer than usual but nothing special, and went to see him in the afternoon. The girl behind the window was very pretty and very young. I don't approve but I also wasn't surprised. I'm familiar with the way he held my arm and fawned over me, and I understand that a man like the doctor appreciates women. She seemed to not understand why I was there and wouldn't get him for me until I explained a couple times that I wasn't a salesperson but a friend. After the third or fourth time going over it she finally said she'd check to see if he was busy. After a moment he came out from the back office, rushing and hurried. I smiled as he walked toward the window. 'Hi, Dr. XXX', I said smiling and reaching my hand through the window and over the young girl's head, 'I just wanted to come by and thank you for helping me a couple weeks ago, it meant a lot and I really appreciate it.' He looked at me for a few seconds as though he didn't recognize me. Maybe he didn't want to let the girl in on our story. I reminded him about the car accident. I saw the recognition come into his eyes, 'oh yeah', he said, 'of course, how are you doing? Ok?' He reached through the window and shook my hand. I handed him the cookies as the young girl rolled her chair to the side. 'Oh yes, I'm ok. No problems. I just wanted to thank you again for your help. You were very kind. You must be a very good doctor.' I smiled and made deep eye contact. He looked at me and then at his girl, embarrassed. 'of course, of course', he stood there for a moment, set the cookies on the desk next to the young lady, and said, 'Oh... well thank you very much. That's very kind of you.' He looked at me through the window and eventually said, 'I'm very busy. Is there anything else?'

I looked at the cookies on the desk, the young girl's manicured hands, the doctor, and said, 'No. Nothing else.' I spun on my heel and walked out of the office. Anything else? Is there anything else? What did he think I was looking for? Anything else? Did he think I went there to ask him out? I'm married! How rude of him. Traffic was terrible on the drive back to my office and all I could think of was how out of line the doctor had been. I didn't even need his help that day, I wasn't hurt, I was just confused from being spun around. The accident wasn't even my fault. The skirt I'd worn was too tight to drive in, it was hot, and I was uncomfortable. When I got back to the office I snapped at the receptionist. He commented, 'you look nice today.' What's his problem? I'm not dressed in anything special. What's wrong with him? I might talk to human resources about him making comments like that. I wonder if he talks like that to the other women in the office. When I got to my office, I was still fuming about the doctors presumptions and so I decided to learn a little more about him. It didn't take long. I got online and searched his name, which I'd done before to find his office, but this time I kept clicking on links and wouldn't you know it, it was just as I'd guessed. He was a pervert. A couple years ago a woman filed a complaint with the Medical Board over inappropriate behavior she and him engaged in while she was a patient of his. I knew he was looking for something from me. I knew he was a deviant. I told all the people at the office about him and told them to be careful; that if they needed a doctor, not to go see this one; that in fact, they should check any doctor before they go. All doctors think they're something special.

I shared the link with them and told them to pass it around so we could all stay safe. Nothing ever came of the complaint against him, it was dropped. He probably paid her off or bribed the medical board. That's how people like him work.

That evening over cheeseburgers and french-fries I told my husband what I'd found out about the doctor. I didn't tell him I'd been to his office, that wasn't important. I told him it just goes to show you, you never know what kind of sickos there are out there. He had his gaming goggles on and was shooting at zombies on the screen as I spoke.

Twenty Dollar Haircut

"But don't forget the songs that made you cry, and the songs that saved your life, yes you're older now and you're a clever swine, but they were the only ones who ever stood by you" The Smiths/Rubber Ring

What's the brass ring? The brass ring probably comes from medieval churches big door knockers. When a criminal was able to grab hold of the brass ring on the front of a church door they could claim 'safety' or like a 'time-out' and whoever their pursuers were had to give them sanctuary and couldn't arrest them.

That may not be relevant. Once I was getting a haircut and the chick cutting my hair asked me if I was looking for a hall pass from my wife. I didn't know what that meant so she explained it to me: A 'Hall Pass' is like a pass to go out for the night and bang some other girl if you want to. In retrospect, I suppose maybe she was dropping hints *("special favors come in 31 flavors, we're out of mints, pass the life-savers"-Prove my Love/*The Violent Femmes*)* but it went over my head. I remember thinking that getting a hall pass from my wife would be kind of a puss move. If I want to go out and get laid by another lady, that's my business, not my wife's, and also that I didn't need to get her 'permission' for something like that. I don't want to, and I haven't, but if I did, I would, and I wouldn't ask my wife is she's ok with it.

When she finished cutting my hair, I reached for my wallet and realized I'd left it on my desk at the office. She let me go on the promise that I'd come back that afternoon or the next day and give her the $20 (I think it was $15 plus a tip). I never went back. I think about her sometimes and I wonder what my debt has grown to by now?

There's a part of me that figures 'fuck it, I'm not going back (it's been like 11 years ago), that part of me enjoys being on the wrong side of the universal scales. I want the debt. I want the bad debt, the unpaid debt with the universe. I don't know why. It's a way of saying fuck-off to it (the universe) maybe. It's along the lines of 'all I do in this world, and this is what I get, judged for $20 worth of bad debt?' It's a strange way of thinking.

Something like Job, the man did everything right and got fucked anyway. Even if he got all his shit back at the end (including seven sons and three daughters), he still lost the original batch of kids he loved first – that doesn't seem right…to him or those seven sons and three daughers.

Maybe I'm thinking if I keep my bad debt on the scales, God won't fuck me (or let the devil fuck me). A silly concern about being too perfect and then being bent over by the devil as the lord looks on waiting for me to curse him. It's only a $20 imperfection, a small debt, and enough to keep me out of the devils line of sight. Maybe I wonder about Jesus who said something like, I won't take my boot off your neck until every last fuckin cent is paid. Maybe I'm testing him to see if, with the life I've tried to live, as honest as I can be, as straight forward as I can be, as integral as I can be, am I really going to get fisted by the King for $20?

Maybe there's some Les Miserables thinking going on. Am I really going to go to prison over a loaf of fucking bread?

I didn't need that haircut; it was just a trim to make me look sharper. I was making a shit ton of money in those days, and

I could have easily paid the $20. Some strange thing in my head? I knew the girl could probably have used the $20 but at the same time, if the measly $20 I stiffed her for rocked her back on her heals, then how the fuck is that my fault? (this was my thinking). Maybe it's a dark corner of my mind (that prefers to stay dark) that enjoys doing things purposefully wrong every now and then. A silent, angry, little rapist who will quite innocently rub my crotch against a lady in a crowded room and then sincerely apologize while nearly shedding a big wet tear. A pathetic sniveler who writes nasty little racist words and wipes his shit on the bathroom stall. That little dude inside of me probably had a hand in not paying that chick the $20. It's unfortunate for her that she crossed my path.

Maybe the more pathetic aspect of this is that if it was $100 or $1000 I most likely wouldn't have even considered not making good on the debt. I'm only comfortable with small crimes. Or if the hair-stylist had been someone who had the resources to come after me in some more aggressive manner, or someone I'd have had to see regularly, I'm certain I would have paid it back without a second thought. But as it was, she was unempowered, and the debt was small enough that I was willing to stick my finger in her eye quite intentionally to see how it would play out. An experiment. To see if there is such a thing as justice.

Now it's true, I've lost many times that amount since then on bad deals, bad hires, irresponsible purchases, and hundreds of other missteps, but I've also made many times that amount and more. So maybe the universe has got even with me? But I'm pretty sure (due to my immature and irresponsible nature), I would've incurred those losses anyway. Plus, the question hasn't been answered, have the dollars and more dollars I've lost since then really been a consequence of sticking that chick for $20? If that's the case, it's a wild fucking west of a universe and one I most likely cannot succeed in anyway. And what about the fortune I've made since then? Do the right thing, do the wrong thing, either way it doesn't matter and either way you're fucked, or you're not fucked and you get more than you deserve and none of it makes any sense.

Lily and Fixation, or Obsession

Someone, a friend, a mentor once told me 'your abilities and potential lie beneath your obsessions'. Obsessiveness destroys my ability to be creative. Obsessiveness destroys my potential...to do anything with a freedom of spirit. I see it over and over. I see it every day while sparring at the gym, every day. I don't want to lose so I am defensive instead of offensive and consequently I fail to take risks, I fail to learn, I fail to grow. It's a major theme in my life, obsessiveness.

I spoke with a woman at the gym today who told me she had gained an enormous amount of weight over the last year and sucked at Jiu Jitsu now. She also told me she'd been away from the gym for the last year. She has an upper rank belt so she had to have been at it for at least 2 years before she took time off, and so she definitely learned some technique at some point, but, it's true, her weight was hindering her ability to perform. As there were only four people at the gym today, eventually I sparred with her. It was the last roll of the class, so Coach set the timer for 8 minutes. She wore out somewhere around three minutes so we sat on the mats and talked for the last few minutes of class. I asked her what happened? Why she gave up training for a year? Her answer was, 'depression'. Then she looked away and said something like 'I get fixated on things and do only that thing...I quit my job, quit going to the gym, sold something (I don't remember what she said she'd sold), and basically fell apart.' I didn't ask her what she got fixated on - probably something in the romantic realm. Then she said, 'my therapist tells me, this is what ADHD does'. I really didn't have much to say. I thought the entire conversation was surprisingly profound and meaningful and maybe even totally inappropriate, plus I wasn't sure what I could say, or if I had anything to add that would comfort her. Instead, I think I said something like, 'well, you're here today', and fist bumped her. I'm sure I came off as not wanting to talk about it, or not caring, but truthfully, I was struck and moved emotionally.

Afterwards, she came and talked with me a little bit about herself. I could see the look in her eyes, a desperate look. A look I easily recognized. I've had it myself. Lonely, scared, someone is nice to you, and the fantasies start. The good feeling, *the great feeling* we get (*the great feeling she got*), when you're in a dark place and someone pays attention to you. The fantasies, the obsessiveness. It's all the same.

In that place of obsessiveness (regardless the object of my obsession) I'm removed, like black magic, from my abilities, my potential, from me. I disappear into whoever or whatever I'm 'hunting'. I felt like she paused when she said 'adhd', and I think she paused because I think she almost said, bi-polar disorder but she hesitated because she thought that might be revealing too much to a stranger, and so she stopped herself after the 'b' sound. Whatever she is diagnosed as; bi-polar disorder, ADHD, or just lonely, I suppose it's all just rampant, pervasive, destructive, overpowering, obsessiveness...and it all has the same effect...we lose ourselves in our own shit.

There's a song by Cheaptrick, *I want you to want me/I need you to need me/I'd love you to love me/I'm beggin you to beg me*, and there's more. These are light and silly lyrics but I also think they're pretty goddamned profound and describe that state perfectly. I'm not ok if you don't like me. I'll fixate on your feelings for me. Not my feelings for you, not how I can make our relationship better, not on anything except 'how do you feel about me', and I need you to need me or else I'm lost, desperate, adrift, hopeless.

My fixation on how many words I need to type daily, health, my sales numbers, on people showing up on time to work, the left and the right. My fixation on why doesn't anybody get it? Why doesn't anybody understand? The list goes on and on and all any of it gets me is lost. Whatever contribution I might make in the world, due to my fixation on myself and everyone else, is lost.

Swimming and Gold

The water was warm enough that I was only in shorts, goggles, flippers, and a snorkel. I'd been out by myself for the last couple days camping on an undeveloped beach and spearfishing in the shallows of southern Georgia. I needed some time to myself so about a week ago I packed several gallons of water, a sleeping bag, some clothes and toiletries, and drove the 18 hours to this beach. I wasn't sure where I was going but East sounded good; the rising sun...new beginnings. I'd never been to Georgia and since it was more or less a straight line from where I started it felt like a good choice. I found this exact location on my phone when I stopped the first night. The destination and duration of my adventure being what it was, unformed, fluid, and flexible, I found myself open to trying a place I'd never been. I figured if I didn't like it, I could leave. It turned out to be good enough for what I was seeking; solitude, spearfishing, and lots of dozing.

It was day three and I figured I'd probably be leaving tomorrow. When I left home, I was feeling anxious and restless. I still was, less than before, but it was still there and in addition I also felt like I was neglecting my responsibilities. I was having a good time on this trip, but I couldn't get away from the idea that I'd left people behind that I cared about. Of course, it'd only been 3 days, but prior to leaving I'd been angry and distant for a couple of weeks. I also left with half-hearted explanations; I told my wife, 'I just need some time alone', I didn't tell her where I was going (I didn't know) or how long I'd be gone (I didn't know that either). She hadn't done anything to make me feel the way I was, but I was treating her like she was the jailer. I was beginning to see that more clearly since I'd left a short week ago. I didn't say goodbye to my kids at all, I left while they were at school. In truth, I felt like I'd been gone for a month.

The beach wasn't deserted, just undeveloped but it was off season, so the nearest (and only) people were a couple hundred yards away. They showed up yesterday, a young couple, maybe homeless, maybe on an extended road trip, I wasn't sure. They had a tent and were camping next to their car. I walked casually past their spot yesterday afternoon, said hi, and continued past for another mile or so before turning around. I wanted to get a look at the people I'd be spending the night with. It gets pretty dark here and anyone approaching in the sand would be silent. On the way back I stopped and made some small talk. They were friendly enough and seemed harmless. They were on a road trip from up North; Maine, Massachusetts, or Vermont, I don't remember, but their license plate matched wherever they said they were from. Nobody is completely harmless, but I decided not to worry about them. They were probably wondering more about me than I was them; a man spending the night in a sleeping bag next to his car napping and spear fishing all day.

I've never been an ocean person. I've never looked out over the water and felt anything sublime. The wind, sun, sand, and the constant sound of the waves; everything on a beach is relentless. The seagulls diving and squawking all day, crabs crawling over everything all night – it all causes me a certain amount of stress. I thought it strange that I picked the beach to spend a couple days – the decision surprised me. In fact, more than once my wife and kids had suggested we go to the beach for a vacation, and I'd always nixed the idea. But here I was sleeping in the sand and swimming in the waves. I'd seen a show on tv about spearfishing and something struck me; the solitude, the thought of being suspended and weightless in the water, the minimalism of it. I stopped at a sporting goods store in a little town a couple of miles away and got the things I'd need. I kept it simple and got just the basics unlike most other areas of my life. In the past when I've taken an interest in a thing I research, over-purchase, analyze, think too much, and then only do whatever the activity is once or twice. A few years ago, I got tired of myself doing this, so rather than try to change the behavior, I'd stopped getting interested in new things. The relation between that and me being here now wasn't lost on me.

The guy at the sporting goods store seemed excited about my adventure and told me to be careful. After he sold me the license and the gear we talked for a while; he showed me how to load the spear, pull the bands back, fire the thing, strap the rig to my wrist, and so on. He talked about how much fun he'd had spearfishing and said I'd have a blast. He asked how long I'd be out and when I couldn't give him a clear answer, he said he had a day off in the next couple days and maybe he'd come out to see how I was doing. I was thinking about him as I sat in the surf and pulled on my flippers. I'd gone out the previous two days and shot at a couple fish but hadn't hit anything yet. The retrieval rope on the spear is shorter than I judged, I suppose because over any greater distance the resistance of the water would slow the spear down too much to be effective in penetrating a fish. The spear needs to go all the way through the body for the barbs to come out the other side and keep the fish from pulling itself free, wounded and lost. A couple times I shot but was out of range and the fish just casually swam off. A few times I just outright missed. Once I saw a small school of fish and thought I could just shoot into the school and surely hit something, but I wasn't out here just to kill a fish. I was really trying to figure this thing out and win one by skill. Working this out was keeping me busy from thinking about other things I didn't want to be thinking about; being a disengaged father and husband, a greedy and out-for-me-only employer, and maybe worst of all a man who, over time, had traded nearly all my self-respect.

I'd gone out that morning and had no luck, but I was still learning. I needed to swim out a bit further to just past the edge of the first breaker. The water got calmer and deeper. There were still waves but the water just undulated up and down in larger sweeps, not the constant rolling and crashing like closer to shore. It was also much easier to keep my head under water and breathe through the snorkel, the waves didn't keep washing over and filling it with water. This put my mind at rest a bit when it came to sharks (and other things) since the water was a little calmer and I could keep a watch around me. I'd seen a few but they kept their distance and I didn't pursue them. Past the first breaker, the depth dropped to around fifteen or twenty feet. I was surprised to see rocks and underwater sand dunes on the ocean floor that the fish were using as shelter. I took a deep breath and started to swim towards the floor wanting to get a closer look at this new world and also check the effects of water pressure. I went about halfway down the first time, swam around and came back up. The second time a little deeper, the third deeper again, and so on until I was able to touch the sand and hang out on the bottom for as long as my breath would hold. There was a school of fish swimming around a little distance from me and some individual fish a little closer. I wasn't interested in taking a shot at them yet, I was enjoying the swimming, the depth, the gentle way the water rocked me, the silence. There were things occasionally shifting under the sand; starfish, crabs, I wasn't sure what, but I wondered what it would be like to live down there.

Sunlight filtered down and sparkled on the shallow dunes that continued as far as I could see. All around me was floating small debris, plankton I assumed, but it didn't make the water appear dirty, rather it filled everything with a sense of life.

I don't know how many times I came up for air or how many trips I'd made to the bottom, but eventually I came to the surface and was content to simply float on my back. Something changed, I didn't know what. I put the goggles on my forehead and looked at the sky and the clouds like I'd never seen them before. Even the seagulls patrolling the water were something new and beautiful. I looked back towards the beach and was struck by the colors of the water, the sand, the tree line, and the sky all coming together better than any painting or photograph. I looked down the beach to where the young couple were camping and felt a sense of connectedness with them. I remembered how leery I'd been of them and wasn't able to understand why. I looked at the sky and thought about my kids, how perfect they were and how much I loved them. I thought about my wife and how she'd been patient and how I'd been ignoring how tired she'd looked. It occurred to me as I floated it was because she was alone. Even when I was there, I wasn't really, and I'd left her alone to raise the kids and face life. I didn't make any big declarations to myself about change, no resolutions were necessary about 'turning over a new leaf', none of that. I only knew that I couldn't and wouldn't go back to the way things had been, not for them, and not for myself. I didn't cry, or scream, but I think I laughed out loud to myself. It was time to go home.

It was getting late, so I decided I'd stay one more night and leave in the morning plus I wanted some time to consider this new understanding I'd been given. Another night in the sand would be good.

In the morning, shooting a fish seemed unimportant and a goal that someone else had come up with; still, I thought to myself, I'm here, I bought all this equipment, and it would be apropos to mark this occasion with some kind of an event to remember. I decided to go down to the bottom and give it one more chance. I put the goggles on, the snorkel in my mouth, took a deep breath and dove. The air and the water felt fresh and new. I got to a foot or so from the bottom and turned upside down to look up towards the top of the water. The morning sunlight refracted down through the water and shimmered on the bototm dunes. The sun was still just rising so I couldn't see it, but the blue sky and the clouds were flickering above the surface. Fish, large and small, were swimming in my vicinity, but I wasn't ready to try for one. I stayed on the bottom looking up transfixed until I needed a breath. I went up and then back down thinking this would be the last time. When I got back towards the bottom, I noticed a dark shape swimming closer and when it came into focus, I noticed it was a shark. Not huge, maybe three or four feet long and effortlessly coming towards where I was. It was swimming at the surface, and I was at the bottom so I don't know if it saw me, it most likely did. I was paddling my feet and arms to stay submerged and not float up. I'm sure it was aware of my movements, but it didn't seem bothered. It swam almost directly above me. How great would it be if I shot a shark on this trip. What a great way to commemorate things. I had a spear loaded already but it was too far away. I allowed myself to float up a bit closer until I thought I was withing range, pointed the tip of the spear toward the underside of the shark and pulled the trigger. The spear sunk directly into the underbelly of the shark and came out near its dorsal fin before the thing even moved. In a split second though the shark darted to the surface and jumped clear of the water as a red cloud started forming around it. The sudden movement scared the other fish that were swimming nearby and they darted off in all directions. The spear is tethered to the gun which is connected to my wrist by a nylon cord so when the shark took off, it yanked me with him. After it jumped out of the water it nose-dived down straight for the bottom, again taking me along. On the bottom it swam wobbling and sideways due to the wound and the spear, across the dunes for a short distance still bleeding until it came to a small pile of rocks I hadn't seen before. There was an opening in the rocks that the shark took refuge in towing me along with it. I definitely did not want to follow the thing through the opening so I was trying to pull the bracelet off my wrist that was keeping me connected but I couldn't get it off fast enough and ended up going headfirst through the hole. The tunnel was only a few feet long and before I was all the way in the shark was already going out the other side. Just as it was exited, I managed to pull the Velcro off my wrist and free myself from the speared shark. I was only into the passage about to my waste with my flippers sticking out the entrance. The stillness after the confusion made me pause. I looked around and was going to push myself out backwards when to my left I saw a wooden box slightly larger than a shoe box. It was man made and very out of place. I knew I'd need a breath soon, but I couldn't help but reach over and open the lid. Inside was full of sparkling yellow gold nuggets; not coins or bars but nuggets of all sizes. I almost gasped for air forgetting where I was.

I reached in and lifted up a handful of the gold then let it drop back into the box. Unbelievable! I didn't know what to think. I had about thirty seconds of lung capacity left before I'd need a breath but I was too stunned to move. Suddenly it felt like someone grabbed me by my ankle and was trying to pull me out of the small cave backwards. I started kicking with my free foot but wasn't able to get a good kick because I had the flippers on. I anchored myself by grabbing hold of one of the larger rocks and kept kicking; whatever had me was strong and wasn't letting go. I looked back saw a shark, not much larger than the one I'd speared, most likely attracted by all the blood and commotion, attacking my foot and ankle. I panicked, struggled, and kicked at its face with my free leg until it let go. I looked back again to see it swimming away and my flipper floating nearby. I started backing myself out of the rocks afraid to look to closely at the damage the thing had done to my right foot and leg. I backed out, desperate for air, and started kicking my way towards the surface and not getting there fast enough. Around me the water was filling with blood - again. I looked down expecting to see my leg and foot torn to shreds. Instead I saw that my right foot was gone completely just above the ankle. I made it to the surface and gulped a lung full of air expecting the pain to hit any minute. I still didn't feel anything, but I knew that wouldn't last. I took another deep breath of air and considered going back down for the gold. My foot was gone, there was a box of gold, there were sharks, I didn't know what to do next. I could feel myself getting tired. I'd lost too much blood; I knew it right away. I took one of the spear rubber bands from my waste belt, reached down, and bound it around my ankle. Could I go back down for the gold now that I'd stopped the bleeding? I didn't know. I was too far out to yell for help, but I could see my neighbors on the beach and I decided to swim towards the shore. I was starting to panic. The pain was starting. I didn't know if I'd be able to make it all the way. I headed towards the shore. When I got to within shouting distance I started screaming for help. They came running, dragged me out of the water, got me into my car, and drove me to the hospital. As they were helping me limp towards my car, I told them I'd been attacked by a shark but didn't say anything about the gold. They thought I was in shock. I wasn't, I was fading in and out of consciousness but in my moments of awareness, my mind was clearer than it had ever been. I was studying the tree line memorizing every detail of the trees, the dunes, the palms so I could find my way when I came back, I knew I couldn't rest until I'd recovered the gold.

Magic

Good morning. Love. I think I'm going to take it easy on me this morning. Try to love me. Or just love me. Move forward. Be in the present. Love.

Light mist. Drizzle. Fell all night. (Magic). Falls now. (Magic). Falling when I went to bed. (Magic). In the morning darkness. (Magic). Out there morning is moving. (Magic). a car starts. (Magic). Early flights pass over. (Magic). The world is not silent. (Magic). The believers are up.

The persona is hard. No nonsense. Pragmatic. Female. She doesn't see the magic... in anything. She's a critic. Maybe a good one. Or maybe good is the wrong word. Maybe a useful one. But she's also a murderer. To her, it's just silly. These poetic endeavors. Silly. And really, not very good. She gets it. The hypocrisy. The power boil...of forcing the magic. Maybe she doesn't get it. And maybe it's not a she. He doesn't believe in anything that isn't spontaneous. She thinks only sparks from crashing boulders catching fire and burning are real. Lighting a fire and tending it are lazy. She thinks the only real fire comes from a lightening strike. Any fire made with a match is inferior. Isn't real. Is stealing. Stealing for the worst reason. Stealing for comfort. She thinks we should move. Always move. She wants us to prove our toughness. If we think we're so tough, then act tough. Rely on chance only. They are brutal...both of them.